SEVEN SEAS ENTERTAINMENT PRESENTS

Daily Report About My Witch Senpai Vol. 1

story and art by MAKA MOCHIDA

TRANSLATION
Liya Sultanova

ADAPTATION
Rebecca Hutchinson

LETTERING
Kaitlyn Wiley

COVER DESIGN
Hanase Qi

COPY EDITOR
B. Lillian Martin

EDITOR
Kristiina Korpus

PREPRESS TECHNICIAN
Melanie Ujimori

PRINT MANAGER
Rhiannon Rasmussen-Silverstein

PRODUCTION ASSOCIATE
Christa Miesner

PRODUCTION MANAGER
Lissa Pattillo

MANAGING EDITOR
Julie Davis

ASSOCIATE PUBLISHER
Adam Arnold

PUBLISHER
Jason DeAngelis

MAJO SENPAI NIPPOU Vol. 1
© Maka Mochida 2020
Originally published in Japan in 2020 by Akita Publishing Co., Ltd.
English translation rights arranged with Akita Publishing Co., Ltd.
through TOHAN CORPORATION, Tokyo.

No portion of this book may be reproduced or transmitted in any form without written permission from the copyright holders. This is a work of fiction. Names, characters, places, and incidents are the products of the author's imagination or are used fictitiously. Any resemblance to actual events, locales, or persons, living or dead, is entirely coincidental. Any information or opinions expressed by the creators of this book belong to those individual creators and do not necessarily reflect the views of Seven Seas Entertainment or its employees.

Seven Seas press and purchase enquiries can be sent to Marketing Manager Lianne Sentar at press@gomanga.com. Information regarding the distribution and purchase of digital editions is available from Digital Manager CK Russell at digital@gomanga.com.

Seven Seas and the Seven Seas logo are trademarks of Seven Seas Entertainment. All rights reserved.

ISBN: 978-1-64827-784-9
Printed in Canada
First Printing: January 2022
10 9 8 7 6 5 4 3 2 1

READING DIRECTIONS

This book reads from *right to left*, Japanese style. If this is your first time reading manga, you start reading from the top right panel on each page and take it from there. If you get lost, just follow the numbered diagram here. It may seem backwards at first, but you'll get the hang of it! Have fun!!

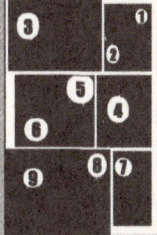

Follow us online: www.SevenSeasEntertainment.com

Thank you so much for reading!!
I love stars, so I drew lots of them while working on this series.
I was so happy~!
I hope you enjoyed reading this sparkly story "Daily Report About My Witch Senpai."
Special Thanks
Manager-san
Designer-san
Family
Friends
All my readers
Maka Mochida

Daily Report About
My Witch Senpai
Story and Art by Mata Mochida

WHAT?! WHO IS IT?!
Right. LET'S GET THE MEETING STARTED.
CLAMOR
きゃーっ
You dog!
IS THAT WHY YOU DIDN'T GO TO THE SNOWBOARDING GET-TOGETHER?!
Umm, about this month's proposal...
They're pretty rowdy over there.
?
[Daily Report About My Witch Senpai] Volume 1 / End

PRESENT DAY.
Yeaaah...
I FEEL LIKE YOU'VE RELAXED A LOT SINCE YOU FIRST STARTED, MISONO.
......
COME ON, PLEASE DON'T BRING THAT UP ANY-MORE...
BUT SERIOUSLY, HOW SHOULD I PUT THIS? YOU'VE BECOME SO MUCH KINDER LATELY!
YOU HAVE A CRUSH ON SOMEONE, DON'T YOU?!
CHATTER
WHAT'RE YOU TALKING ABOUT?
Oh, I-
I'M SORRY.
DID I OFFEND YOU?

THERE'S SOMETHING I'D LIKE TO ASK YOU...
TO HELP ME WITH.
Huh?
RIGHT NOW?
OH, UM...
IT'S FINE!
DRINKS ARE ON YOU NEXT TIME.
OF COURSE.

SHIT.
Have a good night!
THIS IS THE FIRST I'VE HAD TO DO OVERTIME.
I'm hungry.
EVERYONE...
MUST BE THINKING, "SERVES YOU RIGHT."
MISONO.
IT'S PRETTY NORMAL TO MESS UP ALONG THE WAY WHEN YOU'VE JUST STARTED.
HANG IN THERE.
CLENCH
YEAH.
WHAT WAS I THINKING?
UHH...

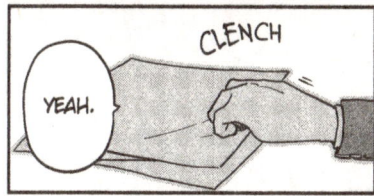

MI-SONO-KUN...
I'D LIKE YOU TO PUT IN A LITTLE BIT MORE EFFORT.
OR IS THIS TYPE OF THING TOO HARD FOR YOU?
YOUR WORK WAS GOOD AT FIRST, BUT EVER SINCE YOU'VE CHANGED YOUR AREA OF BUSINESS, THE QUALITY HAS DECLINED.
YOU KNOW... I WONDER IF YOU'RE NOT SUITED TO IT, SINCE YOU'RE NOT VERY OUTGOING...
SUCH A SHAME.
WHAT THE HELL.
NO ONE'S EVER SAID THAT TO ME BEFORE IN MY LIFE.
THUD

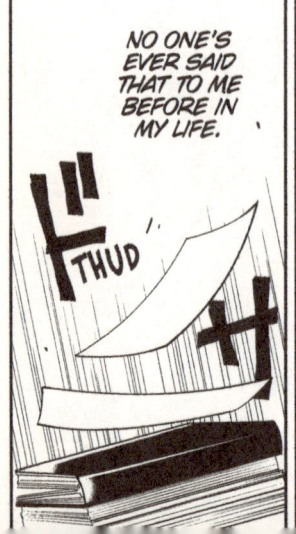

Drinking?
THE NEW GUY THIS YEAR IS SO WEIRD.
No, I'll pass.
I don't think this project makes sense.
DON'T YOU THINK HE'S GETTING COCKY 'CAUSE OF HIS GOOD LOOKS?
BAD THINGS WILL ALWAYS BE BAD AND...
STRANGE THINGS WILL ALWAYS BE STRANGE, BUT...
NOTHING WILL CHANGE IF YOU DON'T SAY ANYTHING ABOUT IT.
YOU KNOW, THE REASON YOU...
DON'T HAVE ANY FRIENDS BESIDES GUYS LIKE US, IS BECAUSE YOU ACT LIKE THIS!
THAT'S OKAY.
I LIKE IT BETTER HERE ANYWAY.
HA HA HA HA!
APPARENTLY BECOMING A FULL-TIME WORKING ADULT MEANS MISTAKES AREN'T ACCEPTABLE. PERFECTION IS REQUIRED.

Bonus Story:
Kouhai-kun's First Year
HALF A YEAR AGO.
HELLO, MY NAME IS MISONO NAOTO. I'LL BE WORKING WITH YOU STARTING TODAY.
I WILL MAKE SURE TO TRY MY BEST EVERY DAY SO THAT I CAN QUICKLY ADVANCE AND BE OF USE, SO...
PLEASE PROVIDE ME WITH YOUR GUIDANCE AND TRAINING.
WELL, AREN'T YOU A LOOKER! GOOD LUCK TO YOU!
BUT, YOU KNOW, PLEASE DON'T STEAL ALL THE LADIES!
HA! HA HA HA HA
OF COURSE NOT.
THAT KIND OF SILLY BEHAV-IOR...
IS NOT IN MY REPER-TOIRE.

Daily Report About
My Witch Senpai
Story and Art by Mata Mochida

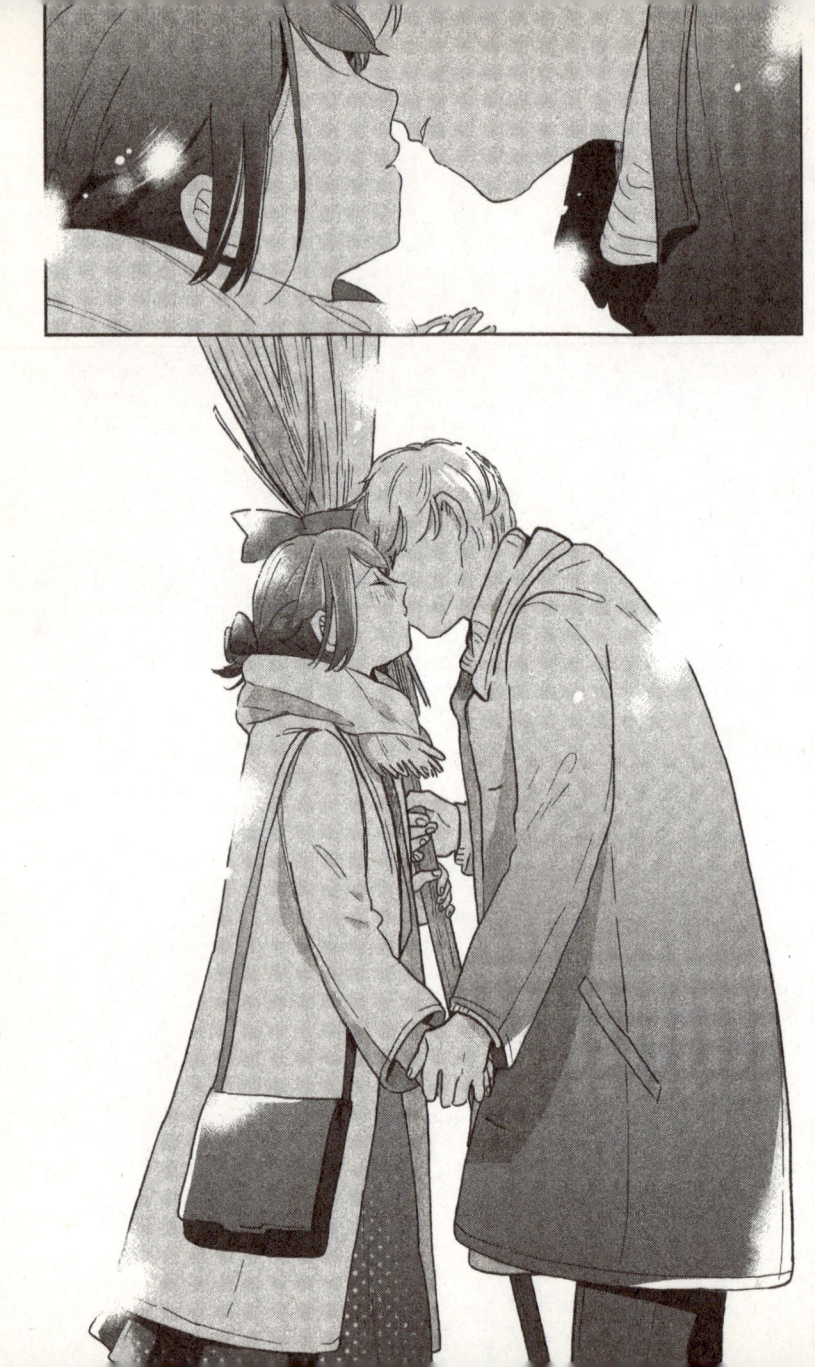

WHOO
OA~!

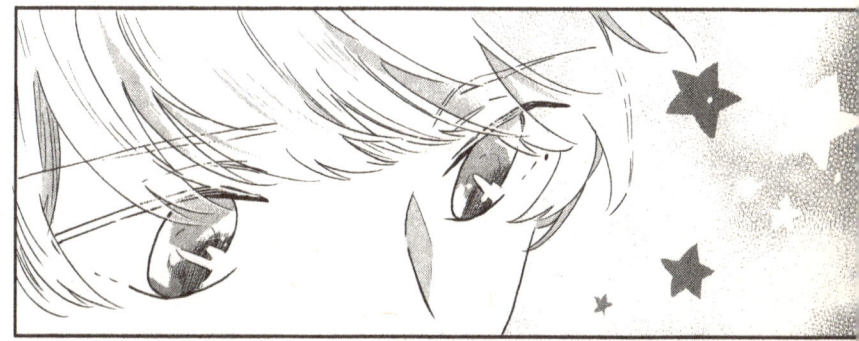

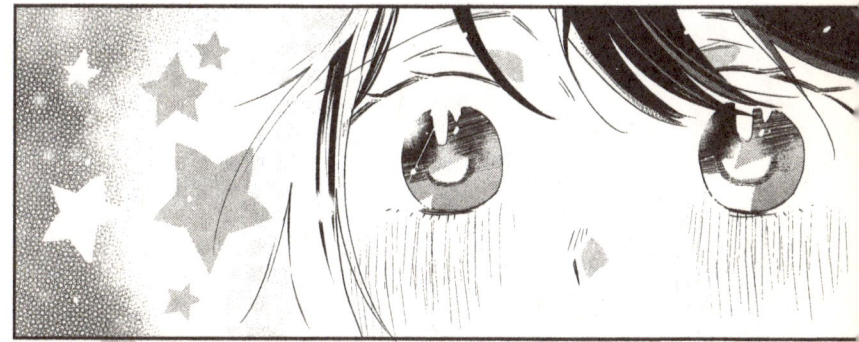

I'M...
HERE WITH YOU, SO...
DON'T WORRY ABOUT IT.
SQUEEZE
The light show will now begin!

I'M SORRY.
I GUESS IT WOULD BE BETTER IF I WATCHED FROM THE SKY.
I DIDN'T THINK OF THAT.

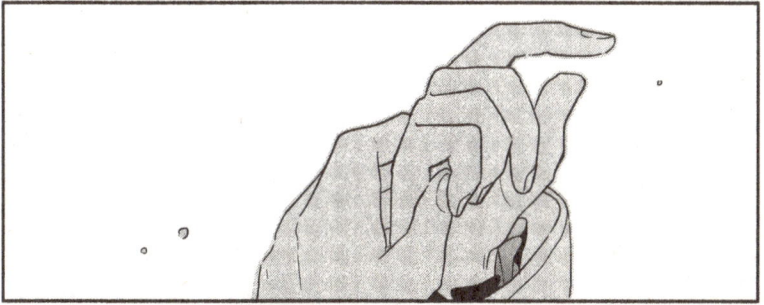

BA-DMP
BA-DMP
BA-DMP
WHOA!
BUMP
OUCH.
HER BROOM GOT IN THE WAY.
SHE COULD WATCH THIS FROM THE SKY IF SHE'S REALLY A WITCH.
HER POOR BOYFRIEND, HAVING TO DEAL WITH THAT.
SENPAI.
UM...

CUTE
Iguana Corner
WOW!
IT'S ALL LIT UP!

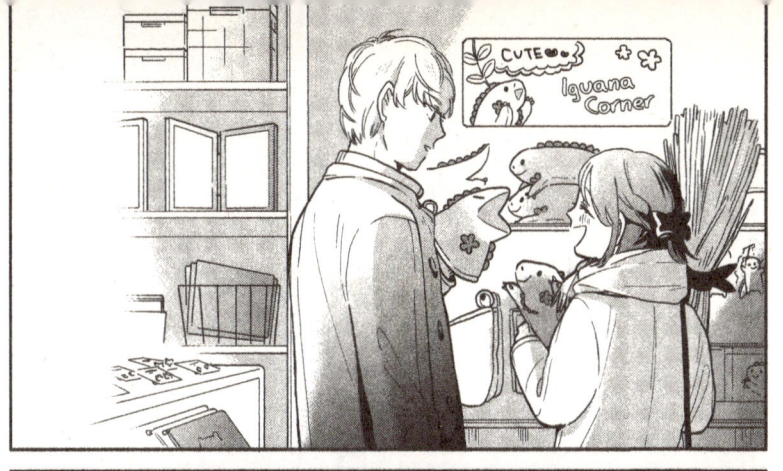

I'M SORRY IF I GAVE THE IMPRESSION...
THAT I WAS YOUR BOYFRIEND.
THOUGH, I'M OKAY WITH...
THAT'S... REALLY...
BEING MISTAKEN FOR HER BOYFRIEND.
NO PROBLEM.
THANKS FOR WAITING~! ♡
TA-DAA!
Whoa...
WHAT'D SHE MEAN BY "NO PROBLEM" ?!

BUT STILL, DOESN'T SHE LOOK EVEN CUTER TODAY?
I WONDER WHY...
AM I OVER-THINKING THINGS?
THIS IS SENPAI AFTER ALL.
JUST SO YOU KNOW, THAT PARFAIT IS A LIMITED SPECIAL FOR COUPLES.
PFFT
HUH?!
IT'S MEANT TO BE SHARED. WHAT WOULD YOUR BOY-FRIEND LIKE TO DO?
WELL UM... THAT...
WE CAN SPLIT IT.

[ENCOUNTER 24]
THAT WAS SO FUNNY!
Hee hee hee!
CINEMA
IT WAS REALLY GOOD, WASN'T IT?
THE PERSON WHO PLAYED KANEDA WAS GREAT.
YEAH! THEY WERE GOOD!
GASP
LET'S GO EAT! I'M HUNGRY!
SURE.
SENPAI SAID...
SHE DIDN'T WANT TO DATE FOR A WHILE, SO...
TODAY DOESN'T MEAN ANYTHING.
STARE

NO!
Oh!
BUT IF YOU'RE NOT INTER-ESTED, THEN...
I'M TOUCHED!
THANK YOU!
WOULD YOU...
LIKE TO GO SEE THIS WITH ME?!
EH...?!
GASP
......
WHAT DID I JUST DO...?

I WONDER WHO HE'S GOING WITH?
SENPAI, DO YOU WANT THEM?
......
......
HUH?
I GOT THEM FROM A CLIENT YESTERDAY AT THE OFFICE PARTY.
LOOKS LIKE IT'S FOR A COMEDY.
YOU JUST SEEM KIND OF DOWN LATELY...
AND I THOUGHT MAYBE THIS WOULD CHEER YOU UP.
!

HUH?
YOU DROPPED...
TWO MOVIE TICKETS...
Oh!
I'M SORRY, THOSE ARE...
UM... HERE!
DON'T LOSE THEM.
OH...
THAT FAILED.
BUT...

BA-DMP
YESTERDAY I LEFT SO AWK-WARDLY...
I WANT TO SAY SOME-THING TO HIM.
I...
I HOPE I GET A CHANCE...
FLUTTER
THIS IS IT!
MISONO-KUN, YOU DROPPED SOMETHING!

I...
SEE...
BA-DMP BA-DMP
BA-DMP BA-DMP
KOMACHI, WHERE'S THE NEXT VOLUME IN THIS SERIES?!
THE FIRST VOLUME JUST CAME OUT NOT TOO LONG AGO.
YOU'VE BEEN ON A ROMANCE KICK RECENTLY.
WHAT'S GOTTEN INTO YOOOUU?
PLONK
I'VE...
NEVER WORRIED ABOUT...
SOME-THING LIKE THIS BEFORE.

CLATTER
WAAAH!
I'M SO SORRY!
ARE YOU OKAY?
I'M FINE!
OH! I CAN...
GO ON AHEAD AND FLY HOME TO GET THINGS IN THE FRIDGE!
I'LL HURRY BACK.
WHEN I'M WITH KOUTA-KUN...
MY HEART BEATS SO FAST. I DON'T KNOW WHAT TO DO...
TO BE CONTINUED IN VOLUME 2

LET ME CARRY THAT ONE, TOO.
!
YES?!
HUH?!
じっ... STARE
UMM...
BUT...
I... CAN'T GET ANY WORDS OUT!
Touch
JUMP

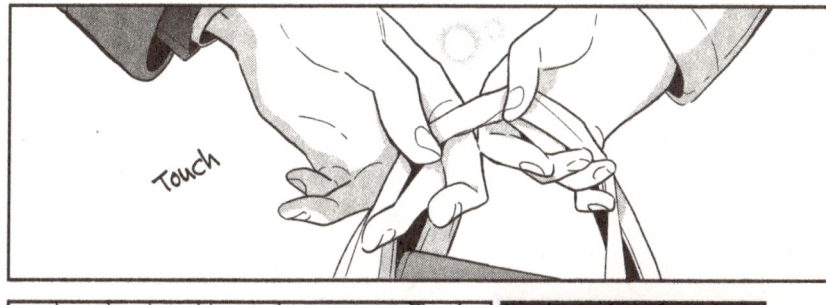

[ENCOUNTER 23]
SORRY FOR DRAGGING YOU OUT TO SHOP FOR THE OFFICE PARTY...
NO PROB-LEM.
IT WAS FUN.
I GOT TO PICK OUT MY FAVORITE SWEETS.
...
SPARKLE
!
FWIP!
Ah!
OH NO! I DIDN'T MEAN TO LOOK AWAY!
SENPAI.

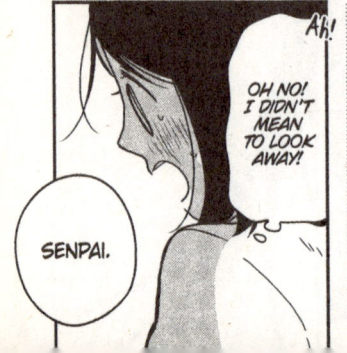

Daily Report About
My Witch Senpai
Story and Art by Maka Mochida

ARE YOU OKAY?

I CAN HELP YOU.

NO, IT'S OKAY. I FINISHED IT ALREADY.

WHAT SHOULD I DO?

I'M SO HAPPY.

OH, COULD IT BE...?

IT'S BECAUSE...

I LIKE MISONO-KUN.

OH... SENPAI...
YOU'RE STILL HERE?
!
HUH...?
WH-WHAT'S WRONG...?
I FORGOT SOMETHING.
I HAVE TO TAKE IT TO A CLIENT TOMORROW MORNING.
I WAS AT HOME, EATING AND WATCHING TV.
THANK GOD I REMEMBERED IT.
......
WHAT'RE YOU DOING HERE SO LATE, SENPAI?
OH! UM...
I WAS ORGANIZING THE STATISTICAL DATA, BUT...
I ACCIDENTALLY MESSED UP HALFWAY THROUGH, SO I HAD TO REDO IT ALL.
WHAT?

...
I'M FINALLY DONE...
DING
SERI-OUSLY...
WHAT...
AM I DOING?
MY HEART HURTS.
CLICK
ガチャ

WH...
WHY AM I SHAKING?
NEVER MIND FOR NOW. I NEED TO HURRY UP AND ORGANIZE THIS DATA!
CLACK CLACK
CLACK
MISONO SURE WAS POPULAR WITH THE GIRLS FROM THE SNOW-BOARDING TRIP. THEY WERE ALWAYS SMILING AT HIM.
THEY WERE ALL SO CUTE!
DON'T YOU THINK HE HAD GOOD CHEMISTRY WITH THAT ONE GIRL WHO WAS INTO HIM?
CLACK CLACK
......
CLACK CLACK
I THINK THEY'RE AN ITEM ALREADY!
CRACKLE
CRACKLE
CRACKLE
POP!

MISONO~!
YOU FREE TONIGHT ?!
YEAH!
WHAT'S UP?
WE MET A BUNCH OF GIRLS WHEN WE WERE SNOW-BOARDING AROUND THE END OF LAST YEAR...
AND THEY WANT TO MEET UP!
PLUS, MISONO, ONE WAS SPECIFICALLY INTERESTED IN YOU~!
WOBBLE
FLAP
WHOOSH
THUD
AH!

?!
HEY, BIG SIS, YOU'RE STILL NOT DONE??
WE'LL MISS THE TRAIN DEPARTURE IF YOU DON'T HURRY UP.
Ah!
HOLD ON! I STILL HAVEN'T PAID FOR THIS YET...
Crispy Chocolates
TE
SWEET
CHOCO
COME TO THINK OF IT, HE EATS CHOCOLATE A LOT.
HE MUST REALLY LIKE IT.
Milk Chocolate
DIDN'T I TELL YOU TO GET THE RICE CRACKERS 'CAUSE YOUR BOSS LIKES SALTY THINGS?!
ACK!!
あっっ
WHAT'S GOTTEN INTO ME?
Yes! A rare one!!
I'VE BEEN ACTING SO STRANGE!

CHATTER ざわ
Souvenirs
Shinkansen Tokyo-bound ←
CHATTER ざわ
[ENCOUNTER 22]
HAVING TEN DAYS OFF FOR WINTER BREAK WAS SO RELAXING!
IT SURE IS NICE TO SPEND TIME AT HOME.
I PLANNED THIS ENTIRE BREAK WHILE YOU WERE DATING THAT BASTARD!
...
IT'S BEEN AROUND TWO MONTHS SINCE YOU TWO BROKE UP, RIGHT?
HOW'S IT GOING?
HUH?
IF THERE'S A GUY YOU LIKE, I NEED TO CLEAR HIM.
AHA HA!
THERE'S NO ONE!
ぽわっ
POP

Daily Report About My Witch Senpai
Story and Art by Maka Mochida

JUST AS LONG AS I CAN SEE HER SMILE.

I'M HAPPY FOR YOU.

OKAY! WELL THEN, SEE YOU TOMORROW.

OKAY.

FLOAT

SENPAI, WATCH OUT!

OH!

SMACK

ARE YOU OKAY?!

YEAH.

......

HUH...?

BA-DMP
BA-DMP

I FEEL LIKE I'VE GAINED A BIT MORE CONFIDENCE.	I WAS ABLE TO SAY WHAT I FELT. BECAUSE OF YOU, MISONO-KUN...

SO NOW...

I'M REALLY HAPPY!

FOR NOW... I CAN WAIT...

DON'T MENTION IT.

THANK YOU!

AND HERE I WAS THINKING I'D CONFESS MY FEELINGS TO HER AFTER THINGS HAD CALMED DOWN.

HMM, WELL I GUESS IT'S NO SURPRISE AFTER WHAT HAPPENED.

FOR REAL?

MISONO-KUN!

I'M GLAD I CAUGHT UP TO YOU...

I STILL...

HAVEN'T THANKED YOU PROPERLY...

SEN-PAI!

"He got transferred to a branch overseas."

"I heard she ended things with Hiwatari-san and..."

"Shizuka's changed recently, don't you think?"

"......"

"What...?"

"She looks so relieved."

"I'm happy for her."

"Should I introduce her to my boyfriend's friend?"

"Hmmm... I don't know. Earlier today, she said she wants to focus more on work..."

"And not date for a while."

[ENCOUNTER 21]

BOSS!

IT SEEMS COMPANY A WANTS US TO HANDLE THE ISSUE WE DISCUSSED WITH THEM.

REALLY?! THIS IS ALL THANKS TO YOU, HOSHINO-SAN. YOU PUT TOGETHER THAT MATERIAL.

KEEP UP THE GOOD WORK!

Y... YES, SIR...!

HOSHINO-SAN, WORK'S GOING WELL FOR YOU, HUH?

TEACH ME YOUR SECRETS!

OH NO, IT'S NO BIG DEAL...

HUH?

BY THE WAY, CAN YOU TAKE THIS TO THE ADDRESS WRITTEN ON HERE?

SHOULD BE FAST IF YOU FLY...

RIGHT?!

THRUST

OH, UM, WELL... I HAVE SOMETHING TO TAKE CARE OF TODAY SO I CAN'T...

I'M SORRY!

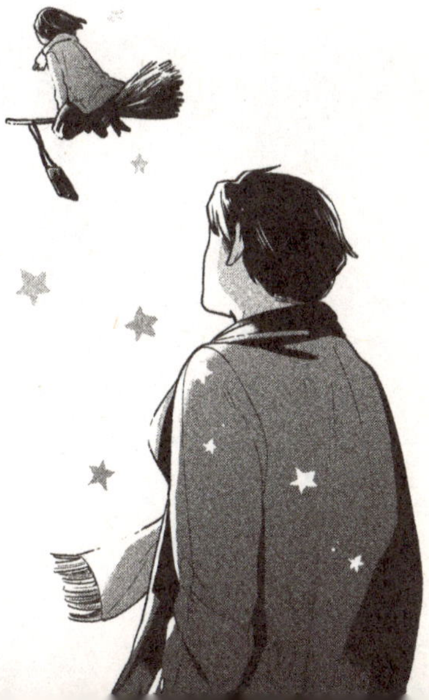

Daily Report About
My Witch Senpai
Story and Art by Maka Mochida

"YOU ALSO... HELPED ME... A LOT, KOU-CHAN."

"THANK YOU... BUT... I'M SORRY."

"THIS IS GOOD-BYE."

ギュッ
SQUEEZE
KOU-CHAN... I...
UM...

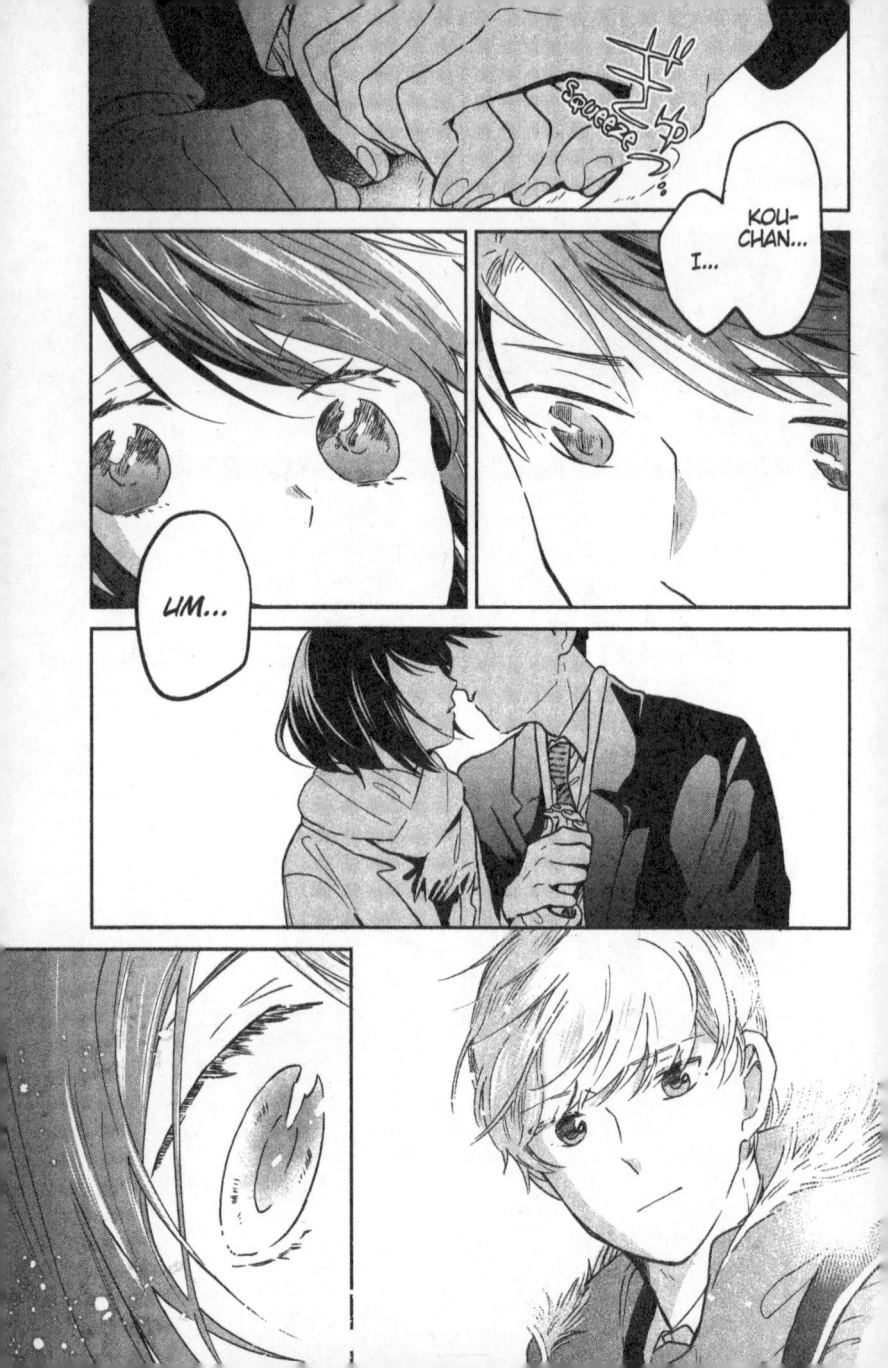

YOU LOOKED OUT FOR ME, SHIZUKA...

AND YOU REALLY HELPED ME THAT TIME.

THAT'S WHEN I KNEW I LIKED YOU.

BUT... I'M SORRY.

I TOOK ADVANTAGE OF YOU AND UPSET YOU.

I'LL NEVER HURT YOU AGAIN, SO...

PLEASE DON'T BREAK UP WITH ME.

"Did something happen, Kou-chan?"

"Huh?!" "Why?!" "J... Just wondering..."

"Oh, well, the work at the branch..." "was harder than I thought." "Truth is, I don't think I'm any good at it..." "So, yeah... Haha."

"That's not true." "You have a strong sense of responsibility, so you worry about it."

Here are more documents for you, Hiwatari.
THUD
Huh? This many...
Hm?
This is what we expect around here.
GLANCE
GLANCE
Are you trying to say you can't keep up?
I heard Hiwatari-san upset a client...
Looks like he didn't place the order and the factory shut down...
WHISPER
WHISPER
Remember Mayama-san? He was here before him. He was the best...
He was a wizard, right?
I was really counting on Hiwatari-san. I'm kinda disappointed now.
an Going Away Party

YOU PROBABLY DON'T BELIEVE ME, BUT...

I REALLY DO LIKE YOU.

I NEVER... KNEW YOU FELT THAT WAY...

I WAS REALLY... SHOCKED BY WHAT YOU SAID.

...

CLAP CLAP CLAP

Nice to meet you.

DO YOU... REMEMBER WHEN I TOLD YOU ABOUT THAT TIME I MESSED UP... AT MY OLD BRANCH?

I heard you're the guru from Tokyo! Our profits have skyrocketed because of you!

Don't mention it.

THINGS WENT WELL IN TOKYO, BUT...

This branch is lame, too.

PLEASE.

...

IF I... DON'T FACE THIS NOW...

MI-SONO-KUN, I...

I SHOULD GO.

BUT...

I FEEL LIKE IT WILL ONLY GET WORSE...

SQUEEZE

OKAY...	YOU'LL FEEL A LITTLE BETTER AFTER RELAXING FOR A MOMENT.

[ENCOUNTER 20]

THANK GOD, YOU'RE STILL HERE.

FWIP

SHIZUKA!

I WANT TO SPEAK WITH YOU ALONE.

...

WHAT... HAPPENED AT THE GET-TOGETHER?

SENPAI?

I JUST GOT OFF WORK.

SNIFF

WOULD YOU LIKE TO GO FOR A QUICK FLY?

ヒソ WHISPER
THIS WAS PROBABLY WHAT WAS BOTHERING SHIZUKA ALL DAY...
HOW TERRIBLE IF IT'S TRUE.
ヒソ WHISPER
I'VE HEARD RUMORS ABOUT HIWATARI BEFORE.
ヒソ WHISPER
APPARENTLY, HE CAUSED PROBLEMS AT THE COMPANY BRANCH HE USED TO WORK FOR.
WHAT?
HOLD ON...
Huff!
Huff!
ドキ BA-DMP
WHAT SHOULD I DO?
WHAT SHOULD I DO? I ACTUALLY SAID IT...
ドキ BA-DMP
ドキ BA-DMP

I DON'T WANT TO BE...
WITH SOME-ONE LIKE THAT.
I'LL NEVER MARRY YOU.
CHATTER
I'M LEAVING!
DASH
SHI-ZUKA-CHAN?!
MUTTER
Wh...
WHAT JUST HAP-PENED?
MUTTER
IS IT TRUE...?
MUTTER

WHAT... ARE YOU EVEN TALKING ABOUT...?

HUH?

YOU PRETEND TO BE A NICE PERSON, BUT...

WHEN ANYTHING GOES WRONG...

YOU TAKE IT OUT ON ME...

AND AT FIRST YOU COMPLIMENTED ME ON MY MAGIC, BUT...

THEN STARTED USING ME LIKE A TAXI SERVICE... WHENEVER YOU WANTED.

YOU EVEN PRESSURED ME TO GO OUT WITH YOU.

THIS WHOLE TIME...

HAS BEEN AWFUL.

BUMP
'CAUSE YOU TWO...
ARE GETTING MARRIED, RIGHT?
WHAAAAT?!
わっ
WHOA!
CON-GRAT-ULA-TIONS!
APOLO-GIZING AFTER A FIGHT IS SO ADMIRA-BLE...
HOW WON-DER-FUL!
NO, NO.
I JUST...
REALLY...
LIKE YOU, SHIZUKA, SO...
HEYYY!
KYAA!!
THIS IS GETTING GOOD!
LET'S TOAST!

I'M SORRY...
BREAKING THAT JAR YOU HAD, SHIZUKA...
WAS AWFUL OF ME.
...
BUT STILL, YOU SHOULDN'T HAVE IGNORED MY CALLS.
I JUST WANTED TO APOLOGIZE.
HIWATARI'S BEEN BEATING HIMSELF UP OVER IT, YOU KNOW.
OH... WELL... YEAH, I GUESS...
FORGIVE HIM, SHIZUKA-CHAAAN!

OH, LOOK!

IT'S SHIZUKA-CHAN!

Kyahh♡

THANK YOU SO MUCH TO EVERYONE HERE FROM FUYUTA TRADING COMPANY!

AREN'T YOU GONNA JOIN US?!

.....

UM...!

WHAT?! YOU DON'T KNOW WHO THAT IS?!

Wowww! No way~!

Do they know each other?

DID HE USE HER FIRST NAME?!

HUH?

CHATTER

AREN'T YOU GOING TO SIT WITH ME?

SHI-ZUKA.

[ENCOUNTER 19]

THEN, I FOUND OUT MY BOYFRIEND HAS ABSOLUTELY NO SAVINGS, SO...

WE'RE NOT GETTING MARRIED ANY TIME SOON.

THAT'S TERRIBLE.

Hmm...

AND HERE I WAS, THINKING HE WAS CAPABLE OF TAKING CARE OF THINGS.

That's tough.

I THINK BOY-FRIENDS...

SHOULD BE KIND TO THEIR GIRLFRIENDS.

WELL YEAH, OF COURSE!

MY BOYFRIEND IS AN ABSOLUTE SWEETHEART!

That's right! YOU CAN TELL ME ALL ABOUT IT WHEN WE GO OUT TONIGHT, SO GIVE ME A HAND HERE!

Daily Report About
My Witch Senpai
Story and Art by Maka Mochida

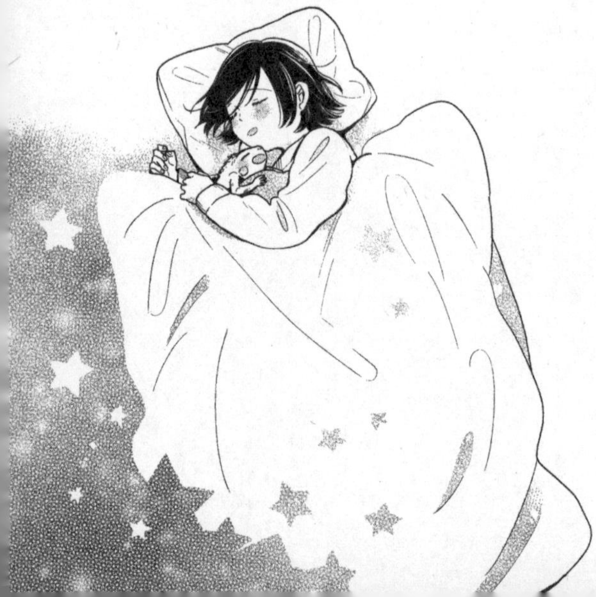

I... NEED TO CHANGE...!

THE NEXT TIME WE MEET... I'LL TELL HIM I DON'T WANT TO GO OUT WITH HIM!

THAT'S THE SPIRIT! LET'S IGNORE YOUR PHONE!

WHAT DO YOU WANT TO DO? WANT TO WATCH A COMEDY?

I LOVE THIS STUFF~! YOU HAVE GOOD TASTE.

Aaaah...

"It should be up to you... to decide."

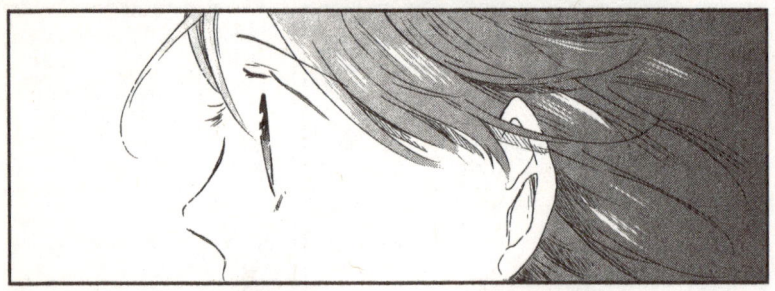

I REALLY DON'T... WANT TO ANSWER AFTER ALL.

CRASH

BRRRRRR

IT'S KOU-CHAN!

WAIT, SHIZUKA!

JUMP

FLOAT

B... BUT...

IF I DON'T PICK UP...

HE'LL GET MAD...!

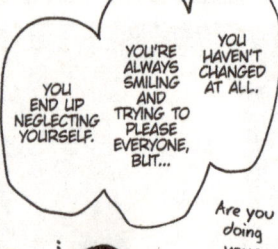

I... REALLY HATE MYSELF RIGHT NOW.

THAT'S WHY YOU'RE ALWAYS...

HESITATING.

OH.

YOU HAVEN'T CHANGED AT ALL.

YOU'RE ALWAYS SMILING AND TRYING TO PLEASE EVERYONE, BUT...

YOU END UP NEGLECTING YOURSELF.

WHAT AN IDIOT.

Are you doing your friend's homework?!

WHAAAAAAT~~~?!
YOU GOT BACK TOGETHER WITH HIM?!
...
I NEVER LIKED HIM!
Your iguana looks funny!
I CAN'T FORGIVE HIM FOR SAYING THAT, YOU KNOW!
Ha ha ha!
HE'S TAKING ADVANTAGE OF YOU, SHIZUKA. LIKE CALLING YOU UP WITH NO WARNING AND USING YOU LIKE A TAXI!
HEY, ARE YOU LISTENING TO ME?!
FLAP
I DIDN'T INTEND TO DATE HIM AGAIN.
BUT I COULDN'T SAY NO...

I can't forget you!
Let's get back together!
Okay!
...
WHY'D SHE GET BACK WITH A GUY LIKE HIM?
HE'S THE ABSOLUTE WORST.
...
THOSE KIND OF NAIVE GIRLS ARE SO DUMB!
HA HA HA HA!
FLINCH
......
Legendary Comedies

Daily Report About
My Witch Senpai
Story and Art by Maka Mochida

IT'S OKAY.
I DON'T GET HURT SO EASILY.
WELL THEN, SEE YOU TOMOR-ROW.
OH...YES. SEE YOU TOMORROW.
SHIZU-KA...
HURRY UP AND GET IN.
...
SHI-ZUKA.
OH! OKAY.

YOU'RE THE ONE WHO WILL BE HURT, SENPAI.

IF YOU DON'T...

SHIZUKA.

LET'S GO.

YOU'VE PICKED IT ALL UP.

THE CAB IS ALREADY HERE.

GRAB

I'M SORRY.

MI- SONO- KUN...

ABOUT THE GIFT...

W... WAIT!

I'm being transferred for work, so...
let's end this.
AT THAT TIME, I SHOULD'VE BEEN RELIEVED, BUT...
SENPAI...
GASP
HOW YOU FEEL AND...
WHAT YOU DO...
SHOULD BE LEFT...
FOR YOU...
TO DECIDE.

BUT...

"Shizuka, show us a magic trick."

"Everyone can't wait to see it."

"You need to come right now."

"You can fly, so it shouldn't take long."

"I have an important presentation tomorrow."

"Can't you do something about my fever?"

"Like bring it down a little?"

"You're kind of useless, aren't you?"

IT BECAME SUFFOCATING BEING WITH HIM.

[ENCOUNTER 17]

I WAS SO HAPPY WHEN WE STARTED DATING...

Will you go out with me?

I WASN'T ALONE ANYMORE...

Since you're new to Tokyo and don't know many people, why don't you come with us for a few drinks?

Everyone is nice, you know?

AND EVERYONE STARTED TO ACCEPT ME.

You've become more talkative lately, Hoshino-san... and even your work has improved. Keep it up!

THANKS TO KOU-CHAN...

MY WORLD HAD CHANGED...

"She's all smiles on the outside, but what if she's secretly cursing us or something with her witch magic?"

"I don't know what to do now."

It's amazing to be a witch, so...

You should be proud of it.

This is something only you can do, Hoshino-san, so...

You should have more confidence.

Hoshino-san is a witch?!

Oh, you never told me!

What if you flew to work?!

What'd I say?

See?

:

THAT WAS WHEN I...

FELL IN LOVE WITH KOU-CHAN.

WOW!

PWOOF
......
I think this should be all right now.
S...
Sorry for touching you.
HUH?!
You're a witch, Hoshino-san?!
Oh!
Um, well.
Don't say it so loud, please.
Why not?
......
CHATTER
Did he say witch just now?
CHATTER

I thought spilling tea on people only happened in movies!

Are you nervous?

You're new here, so that's to be expected...

right?!

Oh... um... yes, I guess...?

It's alright. Don't worry about it.

It's hot today, so it'll dry in no time.

Um...! Do you have a minute?!

...

Hoshino-san, hold on! What are you doing?!
I'm sorry! I'm sorry!
BOW
BOW
You space out too much, you know! Go get something to clean this up!
Yes...
EVER SINCE I MOVED TO TOKYO, I'D BEEN THAT WAY.
You know!
It's past the scheduled time already.
I-
I got lost...
I'm getting off.
SHOVE
Move.
Ack!
The doors are clos- ing.
WHOOSH
WHISPER
Hoshino-san is so gloomy.
She's hard to talk to.
WHISPER
I'M SO USELESS...

"IF YOU WANT TO PICK IT UP, JUST LET ME DO IT."

"YOU'LL HURT YOUR HAND."

"YOU WERE CLUMSY EVEN BACK THEN."

"REMEMBER WHEN WE FIRST MET?"

"THAT WAS FUNNY, HUH?"

"I..."

"I'm terribly sorry..."

TWO YEARS AGO.

DRIP
ROLL

[ENCOUNTER 16]
I'M SORRY...
IT SLIPPED OUT OF MY HAND.
NO...
IT'S FINE.
SHIZUKA, WHAT'RE YOU DOING?!
YOU DON'T NEED TO DO THAT!
YANK
FLINCH

Daily Report About My Witch Senpai
Story and Art by Maka Mochida

?! MISONO-KUN...!

Hmm... SO YOU'RE MISONO-KUN, HUH?

NICE TO MEET YOU.

I'M SHIZUKA'S BOYFRIEND.

HELLO.

SMASH

YOU KNOW YOU'RE MY GIRLFRIEND, RIGHT?

WHAT ARE YOU DOING ACCEPTING SOMETHING LIKE THAT?

AH.

UM... UM... I...

I'M KIND OF GLAD... YOU'RE NOT GOING HOME WITH ANOTHER GUY TODAY.

WHAT?

WHAT DID YOU DO AFTER YOU TURNED DOWN MY OFFER TO GO DRINKING?

HMM.

!

THAT DAY, HE MISSED THE LAST TRAIN BECAUSE OF ME!

WHAT'S THAT?

OH... THIS IS...

SOMETHING HE GAVE ME AS A THANK-YOU FOR TAKING HIM HOME.

SHIZU-KA...

♪
YOU'RE IN A GOOD MOOD.
!
KOU-CHAN! THIS IS SUDDEN. WHAT'S WRONG?
YOU SAID YOU MET THAT DEADLINE, SO...
I THOUGHT I'D COME SEE YOU TODAY.
YOU MUST BE TIRED.
LET ME TAKE YOU HOME.
NOT BY BROOM, THOUGH. BEST I CAN DO IS CALL A CAB.

[ENCOUNTER 15]
SEN-PAI...
FOR YOU.
SINCE YOU GAVE ME A RIDE HOME...
I JUST WANTED TO SAY THANKS.
HUH?!
YOU DIDN'T HAVE TO DO THAT!
WELL, I THOUGHT IT SUITED YOU...
SO I GRABBED IT.
...
THANK YOU!
I'LL ENJOY THEM!

Daily Report About
My Witch Senpai
Story and Art by Maka Mochida

Gotta wait for a taxi...
Heeey! That's so funny.
Let's go drinking again!
WHAT IS... THIS?

IT'S BEEN A WHILE SINCE WE FLEW TOGETHER, HASN'T IT?
...
SORRY ABOUT THIS...
HEY, MISONO-KUN?
ABOUT WHAT YOU SAID BACK IN THE OFFICE...
THANK YOU.
...?
SURE.

YOU'RE NOT A ROBOT, SENPAI. YOU NEED REST, TOO.
OKAY...
YOU'RE RIGHT.
OH, CRAP! I MISSED THE LAST TRAIN!
HUH?!
I'LL GIVE YOU A RIDE HOME!
OH NO!
NO, I'LL TAKE THE TAXI!
I WAS JUST ADMONISHING YOU AND NOW LOOK...!
IT'S OKAY! I'M DONE FOR TODAY, TOO!

Oh no!!

THANKS FOR ALL YOUR HARD WORK! YOU GUYS CAN TAKE IT EASY NOW.

THE LAST TRAIN ALREADY LEFT!

Good work!

YEAH, I JUST HAVE A LITTLE BIT LEFT.

YOU'RE STILL HERE, SENPAI?!

EVEN SO, YOU CAN'T ALWAYS BE WORKING.

YEAH, THAT'S TRUE, BUT...

MISSING THE LAST TRAIN DOESN'T MATTER FOR ME...

SINCE AFTER ALL...

[ENCOUNTER 14]

Hey, Shizuka?

Are you on break now?

We're having a get-together today at a bar. You should come, okay?

I want to introduce you to everyone again.

I'm sorry, we're rushing to meet a deadline right now...so I don't think I'll be able to make it.

PATTER PATTER PATTER

I see. Don't work too hard...

It's a shame, though.

YEAH, I'M SORRY. SAY HI TO EVERYONE FOR ME.

It's so much easier when I can get a ride home on your broom!

Daily Report About
My Witch Senpai
Story and Art by Mata Mochida

FWIP
KOU-CHAN, WAIT!
Whew!
THAT WAS DELICIOUS. WE SHOULD COME BACK.
UM, ABOUT WHAT YOU JUST SAID, I...
ぎゅっ
SQUEEZE
HM?
...
SHIZUKA, GIVE ME A RIDE HOME ON YOUR BROOM.
OH...
SURE.

YEAH.

I THOUGHT HOW FUN IT WAS TO SPEND TIME WITH YOU.

WHEN WE TALKED...

AFTER THAT, WE EXCHANGED NUMBERS AND...

I know!

THEN CAME HERE TO EAT!

YEAH.

SO, LET'S START OVER.

MHM.

UH... HUH?

I REMEMBER WHEN WE FIRST MET, YOU WERE WORRIED ABOUT PEOPLE SEEING YOU USE MAGIC, BUT...

NOW YOU USE IT TO HELP OTHERS.

THAT'S AMAZING.

WELL, IT'S...

BECAUSE YOU ENCOURAGED ME TO USE IT, KOU-CHAN, SO...

"You have a great ability, you should be proud of it."

I GAINED CONFIDENCE...

WHAT?!

WHEN DID I SAY THAT?!

I'M KINDA EMBARRASSED NOW.

....

THE FIRST TIME WE CAME HERE WAS FOR BUSINESS.

Whoa!

THAT'S RIGHT! THAT WAS A LONG TIME AGO.

Ah!
I'M SO SORRY!
DON'T TOUCH IT! YOU COULD GET HURT!
CLATTER
HERE! GOOD AS NEW!
POOF
WOW!
THANK YOU SO MUCH!
THIS IS MY FIRST JOB, AND I'M SO NER-VOUS...
AH, I SEE. GOOD LUCK!
THAT'S AMAZING.
WHAT IS?

[Encounter 13]
SO~? LONG TIME NO SEE, HUH?
WE USED TO COME TO THIS RESTAURANT ALL THE TIME!
...
I THINK I'LL ORDER THE SUNDAY SPECIAL.
DO YOU WANT THE SPECIAL TOO, SHIZUKA?
OH, UM... SURE.
THIS IS REALLY GOOD, HUH?!
UM... KOU-CHAN... ABOUT TODAY, WHY DID YOU...
CRASH
!

IT WAS NICE BEING WITH HER.

You're impossible, Kou-chan.

SHIZUKA NEVER ARGUED WITH ME, SO...

SHE'S SO INNOCENT.

HER REPLY WAS JUST LIKE ALWAYS.

EVEN AFTER I SENT HER ALL THOSE TEXTS...

Long time no talk. Looks like I'll be in the area soon. I want to see you.

I'm still waiting for your reply.

Please, I just want to see you one time so we can talk.

Sorry for the late reply! Yeah, it has been a while. I'm free next week if you want to meet up.

OH, SHI-ZUKA.

I ENDED UP REPLY-ING...

WE BROKE UP RIGHT AROUND THE TIME I GOT TRANSFERRED, BUT...

I STILL CAN'T SEEM TO GET OVER HER...

YEAH.

SEEMS SO.

WhyYYYY?!!

ACTUALLY, I'VE HAD AN EYE ON YOU FOR A WHILE, HIWATARI-SAN!

EVEN NOW, I STILL THINK TO MYSELF...

CAN I GET HIM?!

WHAT ARE YOU TALKING ABOUT?! I MEAN, I GUESS I SHOULD BE HAPPY TO HEAR THAT, BUT STILL!

HAHAHA!

HONESTLY...

SHE BETTER BE JOKING.

GIRLS LIKE HER...

SEEM LIKE THEY'D BE THE CONTROLLING TYPE.

……
WHAT ARE YOU SMILING ABOUT, HUH?!
BUMP
OW!
IS IT YOUR GIRL-FRIEND?
NO, NO! EX-GIRL-FRIEND!
I JUST THOUGHT I'D GET IN TOUCH WITH HER SINCE I'M HERE.
BY "EX-GIRL-FRIEND," DO YOU MEAN...
Uhhh...
SHI-ZUKA-CHAN?!
THE WITCH!
I REMEMBER HER SINCE IT'S NOT EVERY DAY YOU MEET ONE.
NOT SURE IF I SHOULD SAY THIS, BUT SHE'S KIND OF THE PLAIN, QUIET TYPE, ISN'T SHE?
I WAS SURPRISED THE FIRST TIME I MET HER WHEN YOU BROUGHT HER ALONG TO THE BAR WITH US.
SO WHAT'S THE DEAL WITH HER NOW?
DO YOU STILL LIKE HER?

[ENCOUNTER 12]

HIWATARI!

Heyyy! LONG TIME NO SEE!

WEL-COME BACK!

WHAT'S IT LIKE AT THE OSAKA BRANCH?

IT WAS FUN IN ITS OWN WAY.

CLAMOR

MAAAN... I THINK OUR CUSTOMERS WORRY WHEN YOU'RE NOT HERE.

Ah ha ha. YOU'RE JOKING.

Hoshino Shizuka

Sorry for the late reply! Yeah, it has been a while. I'm free next week, if you want to meet up.

VRRRR

Daily Report About
My Witch Senpai
Story and Art by Maka Mochida

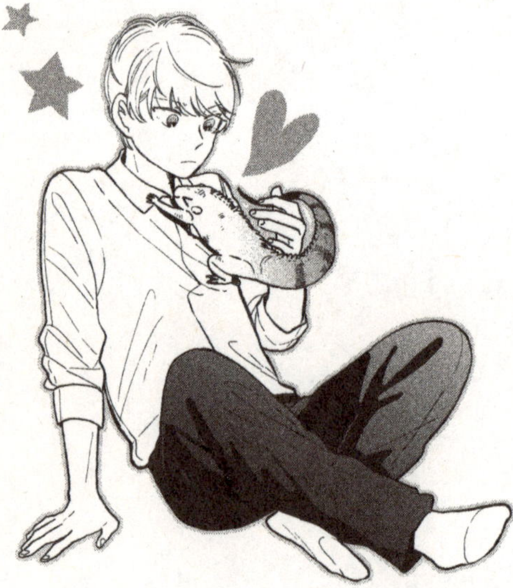

BUT...
I'D LIKE TO GET TO KNOW YOU BETTER, SENPAI.
WELL THEN, GOOD NIGHT.
Hiwatari Kousuke
Long time no talk. Looks like I'll be in the area soon. I want to see you.
HUH ...?

BUT, AT THE TIME...
I TRULY THOUGHT HE WAS A GOOD GUY, YOU KNOW...
ビクッ
FLINCH
SNNRK!
I... OH ...!
Ack!
...
I'LL GO HOME NOW.
I'M SORRY ...
FOR BRINGING UP SOMETHING YOU PROBABLY DON'T LIKE TO TALK ABOUT.

WE'RE ALONE HERE.
DOES THAT MAKE YOU NERVOUS?
HUH?!
'CAUSE YOU LOOKED AWAY JUST NOW.
OH!
YOU SHOULD BE CAREFUL WHEN YOU'RE ALONE WITH A MAN.
UM...
...
SINCE... YOU'VE BEEN IN THIS SITUATION BEFORE, RIGHT?
BA-DMP
YOU'RE RIGHT...I HAD JUST MOVED HERE TO TOKYO, AND...
KIND OF GOT CARRIED AWAY...

HUH?
[ENCOUNTER 11]
KOMACHI FELL ASLEEP?!
ZZZZ...
OH...
UMM, THERE'S STILL PLENTY OF HOT POT LEFT OVER... WOULD YOU LIKE SOME MORE?
NO, I'M OKAY. THANK YOU FOR THE MEAL.
OF COURSE.
I FEEL LIKE...
IT'S GOTTEN QUIET ALL OF A SUDDEN, HUH?
SILENCE
...
OH! I'LL GO MAKE US SOME TEA!!
SENPAI.

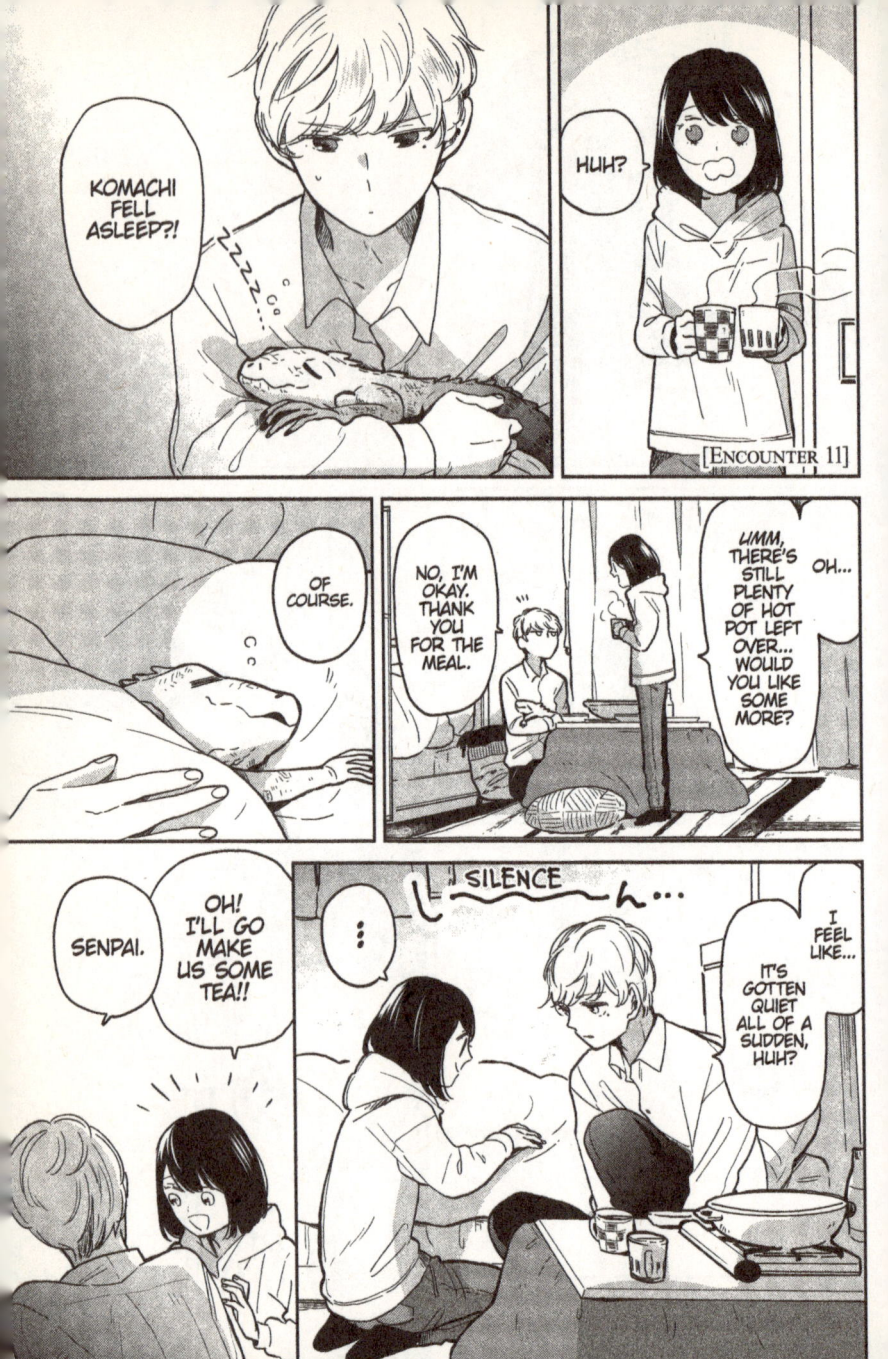

THERE IS A HOT GUY! AND THEY'RE CLOSE, TOO!
WEIRD PET...
WELL, GOOD WORK TODAY.
Whaaat?!
HE'S LEAVING?!
BOW
I NEED MORE INTEL!
WAA WAA WAA!
HUH?!
UM... AS THANKS, WOULD YOU LIKE TO COME TO MY PLACE AND HAVE DINNER? I MADE HOT POT JUST NOW.
OH, AND THIS IS KOMACHI...
Mhm mhm!
HM?
Are...
ARE YOU SURE...?

WELL, I'M STILL VERY GRATEFUL THAT YOU TOOK ME IN.
IT'S WORK! YES, HELLO?
Hah!
I DIDN'T EVEN NOTICE, BUT SHE CHANGED TOPICS...
WHAT?! REALLY?!
NO! THAT'S FINE!
WOOOW...!
SORRY. THANKS...
Handsome
POP
BEEP
SENPAI. HERE YOU GO.
MISONO-KUN, I'M SORRY...
YOU HAD TO COME ALL THIS WAY JUST FOR THIS.
FLOAT~
NO, IT'S OKAY.
YOU'LL BE IN TROUBLE IF YOU DON'T HAVE THIS FIRST THING TOMORROW MORNING, RIGHT?
STARE

BE-
SIDES...

LIFT

YOU'RE WORRYING OVER NOTHING. I'M BUSY WITH WORK RIGHT NOW, AND I LIKE BEING SINGLE.

I HAVE YOU, KOMACHI, SO I'M NOT LONELY.

A WITCH TALKING TO CATS IS ONE THING, BUT WHO'S HEARD OF A WITCH WHO CAN TALK TO IGUANAS?

When I was playing outside...

I found this!

EVEN MOTHER WAS SUR- PRISED.

YOU CAN UNDER- STAND ME?

WE'VE BEEN TOGETHER SINCE I FOUND YOU WAY BACK WHEN I WAS IN ELEMENTARY SCHOOL.

[ENCOUNTER 10]

THERE'S BEEN NOTHIN' FUN HAPPENIN', DON'T YA THINK?

I FEEL LIKE LATELY...

LAZE~

COMEDIES ARE FUN.

?

THAT'S NOT WHAT I MEAN!

I'M TALKING ABOUT THINGS LIKE A HOT GUY SHOWIN' UP AT YOUR JOB OR YOU HOOKIN' THE GUY YOU LIKE!

YOU HAVEN'T DONE A THING SINCE YOU BROKE UP WITH YOUR BOYFRIEND A YEAR AGO.

......

I'M WORRIED ABOUT YOU, YA KNOW?!

YEA-AAH...

BUBBLE BUBBLE

SHINK

FWIP

U'M UFF!!

CLATTER

CHOMP

APPLES AGAIN, HUH?

I... I MADE IT!!

Good morning!

ACK!

THE STAND-UP COMEDY GRAND PRIX IS ON TODAY!!

I NEED TO RECORD IT.

HURRY UP AND GET GOING!

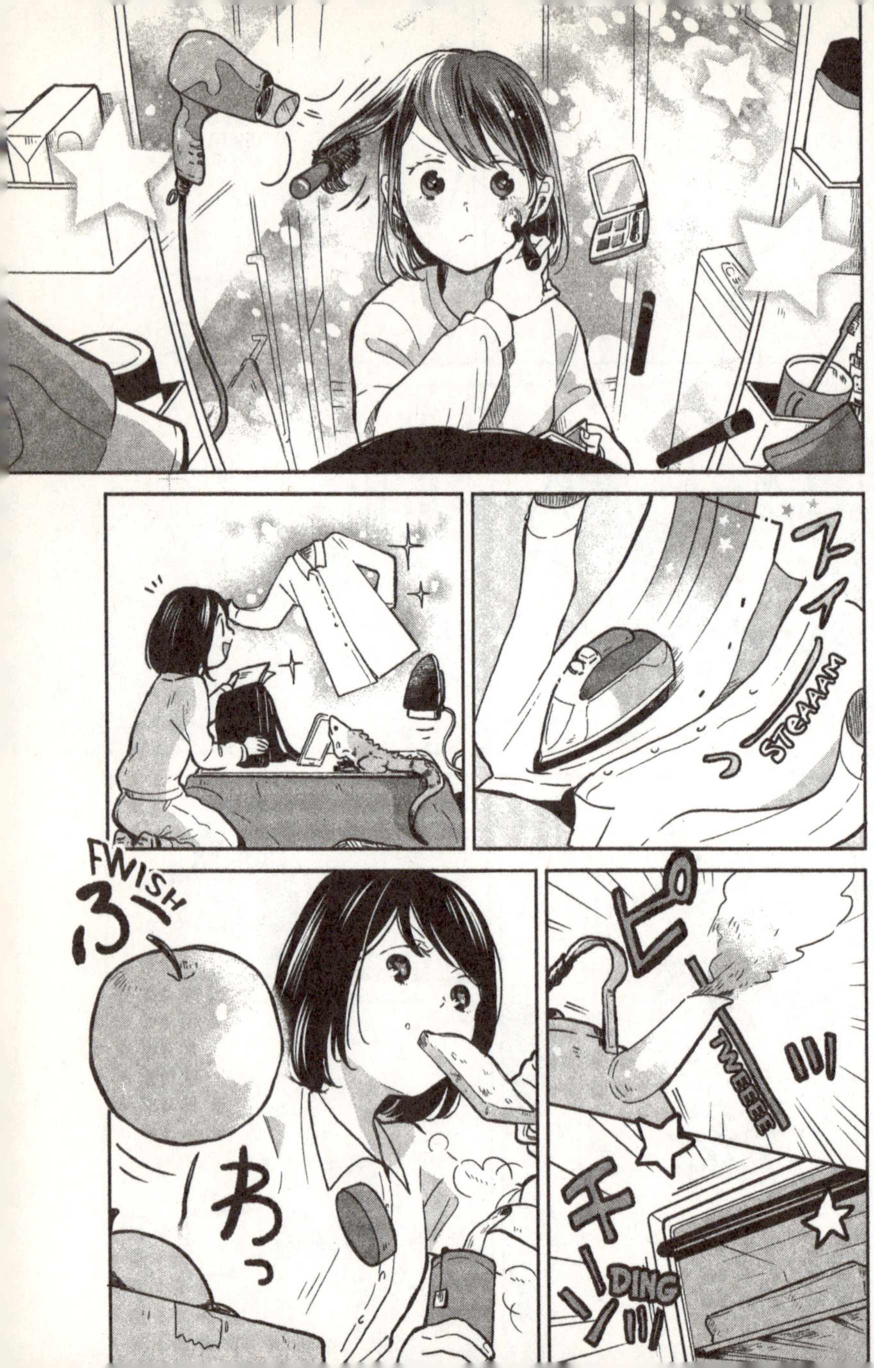
STEAAAM
TWEEEE
DING
チーン
FWISH
ふ
わっ

DASH
THUNK
FLOAT
ふわっ..
SQUEAK
ジャ
FSSSSHH
WHOOSH
PATTER PATTER PATTER
FWISH
TONK
FSSSHH
SPRITZ
SPRITZ SPRITZ
BRUSH BRUSH

TWEET TWEET TWEET...
CHIRP CHIRP...
[ENCOUNTER 9]
CRAWL...
BWAM
HOW LONG DO YOU PLAN ON SLEEPING FOR?!
GO AHEAD! BE LATE! NOT MY PROBLEM!
So sleepy...
I STILL HAVE TIME...
Wait!
WAAAH!
8:57
2 new messages
I ONLY HAVE THREE MIN-UTES!

Daily Report About
My Witch Senpai
Story and Art by Maka Mochida

I'LL BE FINE. THIS IS NOTHING.
GROOOWL
I WANT TO DO THIS FOR YOU.
...
OH!
ANOTHER COMPANY GAVE ME A COUPON FOR CURRY, SO...
DO YOU WANT TO GO?
GURGLE
SO SPICY ~!
IT'S AWE-SOME!

EVEN WALKING WOULD BE FASTER THAN ME...

I CAN'T GET MUCH HEIGHT, HUH?

SEN-PAI?!

THUD

LET'S TAKE THE TRAIN THEN...

I...

LET'S DO THAT.

YEAH.

WHA-AAT?!

NO, IT'S OKAY! YOU MUST BE TIRED TOO, MISONO-KUN!

DA-DUN

I'LL CARRY YOUR BROOM-STICK.

SEN-PAI!

DASH

DO YOU WANT TO GO HOME TOGETHER?!

WOBBLE

AH!

HUH?!

EVEN THOUGH TAKING THE TRAIN HOME IS GONNA TAKE LONGER, WHAT DO YOU SAY...?

WELL...I FIGURED IT MIGHT BE TOUGH FOR YOU TO FLY TODAY AND...

MISONO-KUN?! WHA...?

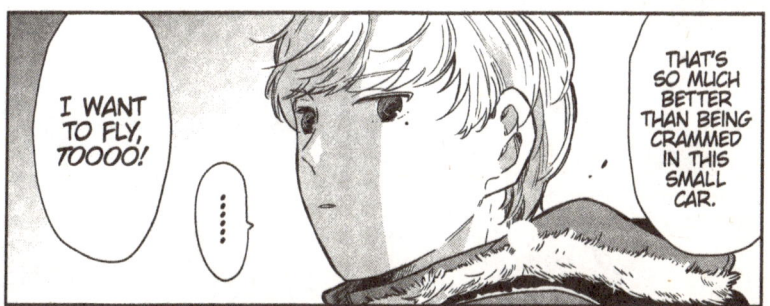

40

WHAAAT?! MUST BE NICE!

SHE SAID SHE'S FLYING HOME.

Huh? WHERE'S HOSHINO-SAN?

So tired.

THAT'S SO MUCH BETTER THAN BEING CRAMMED IN THIS SMALL CAR.

I WANT TO FLY, TOOOO!

......

DASH

Huh?!

MISONO, WHERE ARE YOU GOING?!

COME ON, HURRY UP EVERYONE!

Okay.

[ENCOUNTER 8]

ALL RIGHT, THAT'S ENOUGH FOR TODAY. WE'LL END THE EXHIBITION HERE!

GOOD WORK, EVERYONE!

WE'RE FINALLY DONE...

GET TO THE CAR...

I WON'T BE EMBARRASSED...
IF I'M WITH YOU, SENPAI.
THAT'S GOOD! LET'S GO THEN!
YEAH.
ALL RIGHT THEN-- SEE YOU LATER, TSUBASA.
YOU BETTER GET TO SCHOOL NOW.
WHAT ARE THESE VIBES?!

YOU DON'T HAVE THE RIGHT TO TELL ME WHAT TO DO.

I SHOULD BE THE ONE TO DECIDE THAT.

SENPAI, THE AFTERNOON MEETING IS GOING TO START SOON.

I ATE TOO MUCH AND LOST TRACK OF TIME!

WAAHH!

Yakiniku 29

WHAT'S UP WITH THIS VIBE...?

HEY, YOUR MEAT IS BURNING, YOU KNOW.

WHA...

SIZZLE

OH! BUT IT'S DAYTIME NOW, SO...

WOULDN'T YOU BE EMBARRASSED IF PEOPLE SAW?!

GASP

YUP! DO YOU WANT TO FLY WITH ME LIKE LAST TIME?!

ARE YOU GOING TO FLY BACK?

GLARE

NO.

YO, ABOUT LAST TIME. YOU SAID THERE'S NO WAY YOU LIKE MY BIG SIS, HUH?
CHEW CHEW
Excuse me!
WELL, SEEING AS INVITING HER OUT TO EAT WAS A BIG FLOP MEANS YOU TWO PROBABLY WON'T EVER WORK OUT.
STAB
...
GIVEN YOUR PRIDE, YOU TRIED MAKE IT WORK FOR AT LEAST A LUNCH DATE, BUUUT...
YOU OUGHTA GIVE UP ALREADY.
...?
WHY DO I HAVE TO GIVE UP?

[ENCOUNTER 7]

MISONO-KUN!

EAT UP! YOU NEED THE ENERGY!

WE'LL GRILL LOTS!

SIZZLE
YAKINIKU

SHE EVEN LOOKS CUTE WHILE STUFFING HER FACE...

STARE

SURE...

WHY ARE YOU HERE?

IT'S A COINCIDENCE! I WANTED TO EAT YAKINIKU, TOO!

...

Let's get some rice.

IS WHAT YOU WERE THINKING JUST NOW, RIGHT?

LEAN

I'VE GOT IT!
LET'S MAKE A LIST OF ALL THE THINGS YOU'RE STRUGGLING WITH AND DISCUSS IT WITH THE BOSS!
BONK
......
LET'S FIND A GOOD PLACE, OKAY?!
AND HOW ABOUT YAKINIKU FOR LUNCH?!
IT'S ONLY A LUNCH...
It's a big deal...
OH... BUT...
NOW THAT I'VE RECOGNIZED THESE FEELINGS...
I CAN RELAX, I GUESS.

I ALWAYS WONDERED WHY SENPAI WAS THE ONLY ONE I COULDN'T BE OPEN WITH, BUT...
NOW I GET IT...
SEN-PAI!
WOULD YOU LIKE TO GO OUT TO EAT WITH ME SOME TIME?!
?!
ARE YOU *THAT* WORRIED ABOUT WORK?!
HUH?!
I-
I DON'T KNOW IF I CAN BE OF MUCH HELP.
YOU SHOULD ASK SOMEONE MORE RELI-ABLE...
NO!
YOU'LL DO FINE, SENPAI.

WHEN I'M STUCK ON SOMETHING, FLYING THROUGH THE NIGHT CLEARS MY HEAD.

I THOUGHT MAYBE IT'D HELP YOU, TOO, MISONO-KUN.

I ONLY THINK ABOUT MYSELF, BUT SHE...

THANK... YOU.

?!

IT'S SO BEAUTIFUL, ISN'T IT?

SENPAI, ABOUT THIS MORNING, I--

MISONO-KUN, LET'S TAKE A BREAK!

HUH?

COME WITH ME!

SLIDE

SEN-PAI!

?!

S...

"I couldn't possibly!"

"That's ridiculous!"

[Encounter 6]

WHAT WAS I THINKING, SAYING SUCH RUDE THINGS?!

I'M THE ONE WHO'S RIDICULOUS!

......

AH...NO. I JUST CAN'T FOCUS TODAY...

YOU DON'T HAVE TOO MUCH WORK, DO YOU?

MISONO-KUN, YOU'RE STILL HERE?

Daily Report About My Witch Senpai
Story and Art by Maka Mochida

THAT'S RIDICULOUS!
I COULDN'T POSSIBLY!
FWIP
N...
NEVER ...
FWOOSH
ACK...
Suuure
NOT SURE I BELIEVE YA.
IT...
IT'S TRUE...!
Ugh!
STOP SAYING NONSENSE! JUST HURRY UP AND GET TO SCHOOL!
......!
YES, MA'AM~!
HEY, NO JOKE.
DON'T MESS WITH MY SISTER, GOT IT?
GLARE
......

"DUDE, YOU THOUGHT I WAS SHIZUKA'S BOYFRIEND, DIDN'T YOU?"

"THAT MADE YOU SUPER NERVOUS, HUH?"

"BINGO."

"HUH?!"

"HEY, SIS, YOU BETTER WATCH OUT! THIS GUY'S GOT HIS EYE ON YOU."

"WHAT?"

"NO, I'M--!"

HEY! YOU COULD AT LEAST SAY THANK YOU!

OW!

POW

LITTLE...

OH, COME ON~! IT'S MEAN TO USE YOUR MAGIC ON YOUR LITTLE BROTHER!

I CAME ALL THIS WAY JUST TO BRING YOU YOUR UNIVERSITY TEXTBOOKS!

WAIT. WHY AM I SO RELIEVED?

Phew!

LITTLE BROTHER?!

EHHH?

YOU DIDN'T SAY ANYTHING RUDE TO MISONO-KUN, DID YOU?!

GLANCE

SORRY! WERE YOU WAITING FOR ME?!
WHOOSH
Ah!
SHIZUKA~!
I KNEW YOU'D FORGET YOUR STUFF!
HUFF!
HUFF!
OH, I SEE. THAT'S SENPAI'S NAME...
OHHH, I DID?! GOOD THING YOU HAD IT!
MUST'VE HAPPENED WHEN I STAYED OVER AT YOUR PLACE, SHIZUKA.
BE CAREFUL NEXT TIME, OKAY?
GLOOM
もや
GOING TO HER PLACE...
BEING ON A FIRST NAME BASIS...
GLOOM
もや
HE'S GOTTA BE HER BOY-FRIEN--
ALRIGHT THEN, I'M OFF. SEE YA LATER~!
OH!

'SCUSE ME!
SHIZUKA WORKS HERE, RIGHT?
[ENCOUNTER 5]
UH?
WHO?
SHI-ZU-KA!
CAN YOU GET HER FOR ME?
WHAT IS THIS ABOUT ...?
I'M TSUBASA! SHE'LL KNOW IF YOU JUST TELL HER THAT!
LOOM
I PROMISE!
HO...
HOLD ON.
WH...
Hurry
WHAT'S WITH THIS GUY...?

Daily Report About My Witch Senpai
Story and Art by Maka Mochida

IT WORKED ...!
I SHOULD'VE DONE THIS FROM THE START!
SORRY ABOU--
CLANK
WHIRL
HUH?!
EVEN THE COPY MACHINE IS WORKING AGAIN!
BEEP
IT WON'T STOP!
WHAT DO WE DO?!
PFFT.
HUH?
WHAT WAS IT I WAS MAD ABOUT?
WHIRL
BEEP
WAA-AA-HH-HH!

UM... COME TO THINK OF IT...
COULDN'T YOU USE YOUR MAGIC TO GET THE POWER BACK?
AHA!
OH, YEAH!
I CAN!
CLATTER
CRACKLE
TH...
THERE!
CRACKLE
CRACKLE
SHINE
!

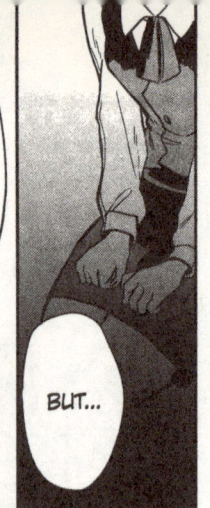

IN THE PAST, EVERYONE FELT IT WAS UNFAIR I COULD USE MAGIC...

SO...

BUT...

NOW I WANT TO HELP OUT HOWEVER I CAN...

WELL...

THAT'S JUST HOW I FEEL.

HEH.

Huh?

SEN-PAI...

S...

BUT STILL... I'LL BE CAREFUL!

MAGIC?

| STAYING HERE LATE TO DO THEIR WORK... | HUH?! | YOU'RE WHAT?! AGAIN?! | YOU SEE, I'M HELPING SOMEONE WITH THEIR WORKLOAD. | AH... WELL... | Actually... WHY ARE YOU HERE, SENPAI? |

THEY'RE TAKING ADVANTAGE OF YOU, YOU KNOW!

YOU'RE PROBABLY RIGHT...

IT JUST CAME OUT...

OH, CRAP.

BUT...

FSSHHH
...
IT'S DARK.
I CAN'T BELIEVE THE STORM KNOCKED THE POWER OUT...
D-DON'T WORRY. IT'LL COME BACK ON PRETTY SOON.
WHEN EXACTLY IS "PRETTY SOON"?
I NEED TO FIX THE PRESENTATION FOR TOMORROW...
GRUMBLE
THANKS TO THOSE GUYS WHO SCREWED UP THE DATA.
GRUMBLE
IF IT COMES DOWN ON ME, THEY BETTER FESS UP...
GRUMBLE

Daily Report About
My Witch Senpai
Story and Art by Maka Mochida

YOU'VE REALLY HELPED ME OUT WITH YOUR MAGIC, SENPAI, SO...
I WANT TO SHOW MY THANKS.
A TASK LIKE THIS IS TOO MUCH FOR ONE PERSON.
AT TIMES LIKE THIS, YOU CAN ASK FOR HELP.
TH...
THANK YOU...
NO PROB-LEM.
LET'S GET THIS OVER WITH.

......

I CAN'T EVEN DO SOMETHING AS SIMPLE AS THIS.

I'M PATHETIC.

I'LL HELP YOU.

HUH?!

NO, IT'S OKAY!

THEY TOLD ME TO DO IT!

GRAB

SENPAI ...?
!
I JUST HEARD A LOUD BANG...
WHOA! WHAT'S ALL THIS?!
CHAOS
I...
I-I'M PREPARING FOR THE MEETING...
HOW IS THIS PREPARING?!
Ah!
WELL...
I WAS TRYING TO DO IT WITH MAGIC, BUT...
I CAN'T MOVE HEAVY THINGS...
NO MATTER HOW MANY TIMES I TRY.

You clearly can't use magic well...
but there's no excuse for poor performance at work!
Do you understand?!
You should at least be able to manage meeting preparations.
Use your magic to set up the tables and chairs in the main conference room.
I expect it done by tomorrow.
CRASH
EEK!
...
CLANG
CLANG
THUD
MM ...!

[ENCOUNTER 3]

GWOOM

I... I'm sorry...

Really! To be making mistakes like this?!

...!

Right.
UM, WELL THEN...
I'LL BE GOING!
OKAY!
GOOD LUCK!
わっ
WHOOSH
WOBBLE
All right. I gotta head back to work, too...
WOBBLE
WOBBLE
...
DID SHE WEAR HER-SELF OUT FLYING SO FAST?!
SENPAI, ARE YOU OKAY?!
I'M OKAY, JUST FINE!

Sign: Station
MI-SONO-KUN! HERE THEY ARE!
THANK YOU SO MUCH!
I...I'M SORRY... FOR THE TROUBLE, SENPAI...
YOU NEED TO HURRY!
YOU WON'T MAKE IT IN TIME FOR THE MEETING!

WHOOSH

MISONO-KUN!

Oh! THE DOCU-MENTS!

S- SEN-PAI?!

Got it!

I'm getting off at the next station.

OH... CRAP.

[ENCOUNTER 2]

I'VE NEVER MESSED UP LIKE THIS BEFORE!

Damn it!

I LEFT THE DOCUMENTS AT THE OFFICE.

I HAVE A MEETING AT ○×COMPANY NOW, BUT...

KA-TONK KA-TONK

WHAT SHOULD I DO? THERE'S NOT ENOUGH TIME TO GO BACK NOW...

THERE. ALL WARM.

STEAMY

THANK YOU.

OH! YOU'RE RIGHT.

YOU'RE WELCOME.

I DIDN'T GET SNOT ON IT!

ACK!

WHY'D MY HEART JUST DO THAT?!

I KNOW THAT.

BA-DMP

H-how embarrassing...
YEAH, IT SURE IS COLD TODAY, ISN'T IT?
IT'S 'CAUSE I SPENT TOO MUCH TIME FLYING IN THE COLD...
I JUST BOUGHT THIS...
BUT IT'S ALREADY COLD.
REACH
GLOOOW

SENPAI IS A WITCH.
YOU MUST BE TIRED, WORKING SO LATE.
YOU'RE OUT LATE TOO, SENPAI.
DO YOU HAVE THAT MUCH WORK RIGHT NOW?
Ah, um...
FURUTA-SAN SAID SOMETHING IMPORTANT CAME UP AND HE HAD TO LEAVE EARLY...
SO, SHE GOT THE SHORT END OF THE STICK, HUH?
STARE
SHE TENDS TO BE A REAL PUSH-OVER...
UH... UM...?
IT GETS ON MY NERVES.
SENPAI, YOUR NOSE IS RUNNING.
Huh?!

OH.
SENPAI.
!
WAH!
ARE YOU JUST NOW LEAVING WORK?
I JUST FINISHED WITH A CLIENT, SO I'M GOING HOME NOW.

Daily Report About My Witch Senpai
Story and Art by Maka Mochida

CONTENTS

Daily Report About My Witch Senpai — 003

Kouhai-kun's First Year — 151

Afterword — 159

Daily Report About My Witch Senpai
-1-
Story and Art by Maka Mochida